T0198774

RAY'S JOURNEY

Through The Eyes Of A Loon Chick

MARIA T. MORALEZ

Balboa Press books may be ordered through booksellers or by contacting:

Balboa Press
A Division of Hay House
1663 Liberty Drive
Bloomington, IN 47403
www.balboapress.com
844-682-1282

ISBN: 979-8-7652-3162-3 (sc)
ISBN: 979-8-7652-3161-6 (e)

Print information available on the last page.

Balboa Press rev. date: 12/08/2022

BALBOA.PRESS
A DIVISION OF HAY HOUSE

CONTENTS

CHAPTER 1

*O*n *a warm, sunny June morning when all the trees were dressed in their radiant green leaves, the water was serene, the birds were singing, this journey of Ray, a loon chick, begins.*

Just a moment ago I was in a warm, safe closed environment, but I'm not quite sure what happened. It seems like my safe place cracked into pieces. Wow, the light is so much brighter, and I feel a breeze. My surroundings are so much bigger now. I raise my head and peer up into the bright red eyes of whom? I'm not sure.

I hear a voice coming from this other creature, "I am your momma loon, and you are my loon chick. I will name you Ray because you are as bright as the first ray of sunshine I saw this morning." She explains that I hatched from the egg which had been my home for the past 28 days and that now I am in our nest. "Ray, it's time for you to get into the water for your first swim," Momma says.

Momma leaves the nest, waddling into the water where she gracefully turns back to me.

"*Hoot, hoot*, come to me Ray," Momma encourages me to join her. I'm not too sure, but I slowly try to make my way into the water. Splash! My tiny body plops and brrrr the water is so cold. I begin to bob up and down.

"That's right, Ray, you did it! Welcome to Pawtuckaway Lake," she says.

"Oooh, I'm scared," I exclaim, bobbing up and down on the ripples of the water, "I don't like this insecure feeling."

"It's okay, Ray, you'll get the hang of it very soon," Momma comforts me as she swims close, lowering her wing into the water next to me, and gently easing me up onto her back.

I see another loon approaching us. "Hey, Momma, who is that?" I ask.

"Ray, that is your dad. He was out on the lake feeding and capturing food for you," Momma explains and then calls out to my dad. *Hoot,hoot, hoot.*

Dad swims closer to us with a small minnow in his mouth. "Ray, this one's for you," he says. Dad swims closer to me, and I open my mouth. He releases the minnow, and I gobble it down.

"Yum, that was good. May I have another one?" I ask.

"I'm going to go catch myself some lunch," says Momma as she dives down into the lake to catch some fish while I plop back into the water.

Loons can dive 30 to 150 feet down and can hold their breath for up to 3 minutes.

I'm ok with the plop this time because my dad feeds me another fish he has in his mouth, and I feel safe. I paddle around slowly and watch as my momma and my dad take turns diving and coming back up with all sorts of fish, big and small, for us to eat.

Now that our bellies are full, Momma and Dad begin **preening** themselves.

Preening is cleaning their feathers with their bills to disperse the oils from their skin. This helps with buoyancy, which is the ability to float, and it also helps to protect from the cold water.

I continue floating around trying out my legs and web-like feet to swim. The sun is shining bright and the warmth from above feels so good. I am just beginning to relax when I suddenly feel a tug on my foot.

"Peep! Peep! Peep!" I cry out. My parents are alarmed and quickly come to help me. Dad lets out a **tremolo**, "Danger, Danger!" and dives down into the water to chase away whatever was under there grabbing my foot.

A tremolo is a call that is a warning of danger. It usually consists of four or five rapid calls in a series.

Momma lowers her wing again and quickly helps me onto her back. Once my dad surfaces, I look at him and wonder what happened.

"Ray, that was a snapping turtle that was trying to eat you for lunch," he explains, "Snapping turtles are one of our predators that live in the water." I'm frightened, so I stay on my momma's back for safety and slowly fall asleep tired from all of the excitement.

I'm abruptly woken by a *boom* above my head and *crash*, a bright flash of light that zigzags in the sky. The down pouring rain hits me like ice cold drops. Momma lifts her wing over my body to protect me from the weather. Yikes! My body is paralized with fear of the unknown.

"Ray, the loud boom is just thunder and the crash is lightning, but it will all pass soon," Momma assures me.

She swims us closer to an island with overhanging trees. That helps me feel a little better. We remain there until the storm slowly begins to subside and the sound of thunder fades.

"Momma, why didn't we just go back to our nest during the storm?" I ask.

"Once we leave our nest, we live in the water. That is why we have webbed feet that are set far back on our bodies. We are born to dive and swim," she explains.

Loons only return to land to build a nest and to lay and incubate their eggs.

As I think about the day, I finally fall back to sleep on my momma's back.

CHAPTER 2

Oh no! I wake to a loud scary splashing sound beside me. This time, I'm happy to see that it is just my dad. He has a nice perch that he is working on eating for breakfast.

"Momma, I heard so many sounds throughout the night. What made all of those noises?" I ask.

"What you heard, Ray, may have been wildlife that lives all around the lake. You probably heard the owls hooting, the fisher cats screeching, and the raccoons scuffling around the leaves. You may have also heard the sounds of people that live on the lake or that are at the campground talking or even playing music," Momma explains before she dives down to start our morning feeding.

I am getting better at using my feet to paddle around. I hold my breath and slowly poke my head below the water. I'm amazed that I can completely submerge my body and use my legs to swim underwater.

I'm so excited when I come to the surface and take a big breath of air. "I did it!" I call out in excitement. I'm already growing stronger. I hear my tummy grumble with hunger. In all of my excitement over learning to dive, I forgot our original mission. Momma comes up from under the water with a nice perch, but she does not share because the fish is too big for me. Dad comes up with a minnow and feeds me. That is more my size. I continue to practice my diving skills in between Momma and Dad feeding me. I'm getting more confident and try my luck at catching a fish. I hold my breath and dive.

Everything looks so different under the water. I finally see a minnow and open my bill to try and catch it. Good grief! It got away, and I'm out of air! I pop up from under the water and gulp the fresh air.

That was an exhausting adventure for one day, but I continue paddling around while being fed until my tummy is full. Momma and Dad begin their preening session. I attempt to do the same, however, I'm a little clumsy at moving my body in the different ways they do. I'm also not as majestic-looking as they are. Momma and Dad spread their wings open wide and flap them. They point their bills to the sky, slowly lifting their bodies to the surface of the water, and gently lowering back down. They then use their bills to separate and shed some of their feathers. I, on the other hand, just basically flop around and try to mimic their behaviors while looking a bit silly.

"Ray, it will take a little time for you to master that skill as well as other skills like feeding yourself. Just be patient. You'll learn," Momma and Dad assure me.

Weeks pass and I'm so excited that I have learned to catch fish and feed myself. Momma and Dad are so proud of me, and after we've had our meals, I can preen myself without looking goofy.

Loon chicks transform from helpless little gray feathered hatchlings that weigh about 4 ounces to black and white feathered juvenile loons weighing almost 6 pounds.

My parents encourage me to become even more independent. They both go about their daily routines and leave me to explore on my own. I enjoy this time being adventurous. *Aha*, I spy a nice fish and dive down toward it. I open my bill and *hooray*! I got it. I surface with it and struggle at first, but I manage to swallow the whole fish. It was a good size, and my belly is satisfied for now.

The loon's common diet consists of minnows, yellow perch, bass, sunfish, crayfish, crabs, snails, and even insects. On occasion adult loons will even eat baby ducklings.

I begin preening myself, but then I hear my parents both sounding the tremolo call. Oh no! I'm not sure what to do. I freeze and wait for their direction. Momma swims close to me and calls to Dad with a *hoot, hoot, hoot*, letting him know that I am safe. "Momma? Dad? What just happened?" I ask.

My parents reply, "Ray, that was an eagle, a predator that comes from the sky. We have to watch out because they can swoop down fast to capture us."

Eagles are able to see their prey from 1 mile above the water. They fold their wings to swoop down quickly in a stealth-like manner. They can snatch loons up with their talons. Eagles feed on fish and all kinds of waterfowl including loons and ducks.

In July and August summer storms come and go, and I am now not as scared of thunder and lightning as I used to be.

CHAPTER 3

After the heat of August, the weather changes from warm and sunny to cooler and windy. The days begin to grow shorter. Even the water temperature begins to get a bit chilly. We are all out searching for a meal, when I notice something that looks appetizing cruising in. I begin my pursuit. Dad is nearby keeping an eye on me when he realizes it is not a meal. It is a dangerous hook coming from a fishing line!

Dad sounds the tremolo call, and I immediately stop pursuit and swim towards him. "That was a fishing line and hook that people use to catch fish, but it is very dangerous to us. The hook can get stuck in our throats, and the fishing line can entangle our bodies causing severe injuries or even death," Dad explains, "Ray, please always remember this important lesson."

I open my eyes wide, "Dad, that is so scary! I will never forget this lesson!"

I notice the leaves on the trees begin to turn from green to different shades of yellow and red. "Momma, what is happening to the trees? Why is the weather getting cooler?" I ask.

"This is the season of the year that is called autumn, and it is also a time when your dad will soon leave us to migrate. We will move from one home to another because of the season change. When the winter arrives, the lake will freeze, and we will not be able to swim and feed ourselves. The ocean where we migrate to does not freeze, and we can swim, dive, and fish all winter long. Your dad will fly to the ocean first. I'll stay with you for a while, but then I will fly to the ocean as well," Momma explains.

"Momma, I don't want you to leave!" I cry, "Why do you and Dad leave sooner?"

Momma explains, "We must migrate before you because we are adults. We must make it safely to the ocean so we can **molt** our summer flight feathers for our new flight feathers to grow in. All of you youngsters don't have to worry about this transformation until your second year of life, so you can stay on your home lake longer."

Molt means to shed their feathers. Loons molt their summer flight feathers from the previous year while on the ocean. During this time, they are completely flightless for close to a month. "Momma, how am I going to make that long journey to the ocean alone?" I ask.

Momma encourages me once again, "You must practice your flying skills to be ready for migration. You'll need to practice on a big stretch of open water and flap your wings really hard. Then your body will lift out of the water, like magic. You'll also need to learn how to land on the water. You will have to hold your wings very high over your back so you don't get hurt. You will slowly skim the top of the water and glide into a landing. It'll be fun. You'll see. Let me show you."

Loon bones are very dense, giving a heavy body weight. Males weigh from 7-17 lbs and females weigh from 5.5-14 lbs. They need at least 100 yards of water to almost run and propel their wings to take flight.

Momma gracefully speeds up as if she's almost running on the surface of the water and propels her wings. Soon she is high above the lake. "Hey, that was amazing! Momma, that looks so fun!" I say as I watch Momma land not too far from me.

"Okay, Ray, now you try," Momma commands. I paddle my feet and flap my wings and work vigorously over and over again, but I am not successful.

"Momma, this is the most difficult skill I must learn," I whine.

"Ray, just practice several times each day, and it will happen," Momma reassures me.

I take Momma's advice and practice flying skills for days. Just when I think it's impossible…*whoa*, I begin to lift up higher and higher into the sky! I flap my wings and enjoy the fresh cool air as I glide into the wind. I feel so free and in control. I'm flying! I make a short flight over the lake, and I'm so exhilarated. Then, I realize I'm getting a bit tired and decide I should now try out my landing skills.

I begin to descend. I hold my wings very high over my back just like Momma said. I skim the water and slowly glide into a pretty good landing. I'm proud of myself and have worked up an appetite. Momma greets me, "Ray, you did a great job! You just have to keep practicing, and you will safely make the journey to the ocean."

Dad joins us, "Ray, I was watching you from a distance. Keep up the good work, and you will do fine."

CHAPTER 4

The day arrives when my dad bids Momma and me farewell and takes flight. He circles over the lake for the last time this year and leaves us with the sounds of his tremolo, this time used as a flight call. He then begins his journey to the seacoast of New Hampshire for the winter months. "Momma, I'm so sad. I will miss dad," I cry.

"It won't be long before we all join each other again," Momma consoles me.

For the next few weeks, Momma and I go about our daily routines. I notice the colorful leaves that were on the trees are now floating on the surface of the water and scattered across the land surrounding the lake. It's October and everything seems to be more tranquil. There are not as many people or boats in the water. The air is so calming. The water on the lake at times is as still as glass and reflects the images of the surrounding land.

One day Momma and I are fishing close to the beach shore. I'm so curious to feel what it would be like for my feet to be on the sand. "Momma, can I try my legs on land?"

"Of course, Ray, go for it," she encourages, "I will float here and watch you." I creep ever so slowly towards the shore and begin to drag my body onto the sand. I get almost two feet onto land but turn around and head back to the water and paddle to my momma.

"I'm glad I tried that, but now I understand how hard it is to move around on land," I say.

On a very cold, cloudy day, Momma tells me that time has come for her to leave me and make her journey to the ocean to join my dad. "I know, Momma. I will be okay. You and Dad have helped me learn so many skills. I have confidence that I will be able to take care of myself and stay safe," this time I am reassuring Momma.

Momma hoots to me and takes flight. I watch as her body begins to look smaller and smaller, and then she is just a black speck in the sky. I feel a tear falling from my eye and slowly rolling down my face, but I find comfort in knowing that I will join Momma and Dad soon.

CHAPTER 5

On an evening shortly after Momma's departure, I'm sleeping peacefully on the surface of the water with my head tucked into my feathers. Suddenly, I feel my entire body being covered and enclosed by something I have never experienced in my life. I'm nervous and frightened and don't know what to expect, so I begin to **wail**.

A wail is a call loons make when they feel threatened or are looking for each other.

I hear a calm, slow voice say, "It's okay young loon. I mean you no harm. My name is John and I am from the Loon Preservation Committee (LPC) . Our mission is to study your species, educate the public, and help your population to increase. I'm just going to band your legs with a series of 2 colored bands on each leg. We will use these to monitor you and learn more about your migration and breeding habits."

I then feel warm hands holding my body and a slight tug on one leg and a small clamp, but I am okay. I feel the same on my other leg. In a matter of minutes, I'm back in the water where I belong. I hear John's voice, "Thank you for your patience young loon. I wish you a good life." I quickly make my way onto the lake only turning to look back at John and give him a *hoot, hoot*. I feel privileged to have been selected for banding knowing that it will educate the public about helping the loon population.

http://www.loon.org **(LPC) Loon Preservation Committee**

I continue flying and landing daily until I notice the water on the lake is freezing, and I'm losing a lot of my feeding grounds. As I take flight and fly over my home lake, I am not quite able to make a safe landing, so I make my decision to begin my journey to the ocean. I, like my dad, make one last flight over the lake and give a tremolo call. Then seacoast, here I come.

Whew! I've only been flying for hours, but it feels like an eternity, and I'm hungry. My belly is screaming for food, so I know I must rest.

As I fly, I look for open lake waters. I spot a lake and start to descend. I hope I can make a safe landing on the unfrozen part. *Splash*! "I did it!" I call out triumphantly. I am so hungry I need to find a nice fat bass, so I begin peering beneath the surface. I see one, and I hurry to capture my meal. " Oh boy! I got him!" I am so proud of myself for being successful on the first try. Now my belly is so satisfied that it's time to preen myself.

Wait! What's that noise? I listen and hear the sounds of other loons calling, so I head in their direction. I come upon a group of other juvenile loons socializing and congregating. They must be preparing for their journey to the ocean too. I greet them with a *hoot, hoot,* and we all splash around playfully. We also practice taking flight and landing. I feel very comfortable with one particular loon, so I get closer and introduce myself.

"Hi, I'm Ray. What's your name?" I ask.

"Umm, my name is Selina. I'm from Lake Massabesic in New Hampshire," the young loon responds.

"Wow! I'm from Pawtuckaway Lake in New Hampshire. It's so nice to meet another loon from close to my home," I exclaim. We go about our day and continue to eat, preen, and rest. At the end of the day, I ask, "Selina, would you like to make the rest of the journey to the ocean together?"

Selina replies, "Oh, yes. I think the company would be great!" We then find a cozy spot on the lake, tuck our bills into our feathers, and slip into a restful sleep for the night.

CHAPTER 6

The sun begins to rise showing off its beautiful early morning colors of coral and violet. Selina and I decide it is time to fill our bellies and then take flight to continue our trek to the ocean. "Selina, I caught a big sunfish to share with you if you'd like," I tell my new friend.

"That sounds great. I am pretty hungry," she replies. We both work on eating our meal and do a bit of preening before we continue our journey.

I make my way across the top of the water and ascend up into the sky. Selina joins me. We vocalize in flight. It is so nice to have a flying companion. We continue flying for quite a while until I see what looks like a body of water that is so much bigger than my home lake. "Selina do you see that?" I ask.

"Yes, I do!" she replies.

Below us is the most amazing body of water I have ever seen. The choppy waves are a deep aqua blue. My instincts tell me that this is the ocean. I call out to Selina, and I begin my landing, but the waves make landing very difficult. I try to steady myself, and I am just in time to see Selina make her descent into the ocean. She is smaller than me and has a much more graceful landing, however, she also has a difficult time steadying herself on the waves.

This water is so different from what I'm used to. It is colder and has a different taste. Is this the salt Momma told me about? I can taste the difference.

I begin to peer into the water to look for food, but it is so blurry. Selina is also feeling a little uneasy. I do my best and try to catch something to eat, and somehow I capture a fish, and I swallow it down. Selina is not successful, so I continue searching for food. I catch and bring her a fish. She breaks it apart and manages to swallow some, however, she is not at all pleased with the flavor. " Ray, that was nothing like what I'm used to eating. It was kind of yucky, but thank you for sharing with me," she says. As we swim around, I see other wildlife in the water, but they are not loons. Most of them are seagulls. I try to steady myself on the surface of the water, but it is difficult. I guess with time, Selina and I will become accustomed to our new surroundings.

On the ocean, a loon's diet mostly consists of flounder, herring, bass, and crustaceans. Loons have a salt gland to excrete excess salt they ingest while feeding on the ocean creatures.

Night arrives soon, and I try to tuck my head into my feathers to stay warm as I sleep, and Selina does the same. The sounds on the ocean are much more extreme than the sounds on my home lake. I hear great loud rumbling sounds coming from large shapes moving in the water. I can even feel the vibrations coming from them. I can hear eerie sounds coming from tall fixtures with bright lights on the top of them. I need to find my momma and dad, so they can tell me all about what I'm hearing and seeing. I hope to reunite with them soon.

CHAPTER 7

I'm awakened by a familiar call. I'm so excited because I feel like it may be one of my parents. I respond to the call with a *hoot, hoot, hoot*. Suddenly before my eyes, I see a loon I recognize. Could it be? The loon responds back to me *hoot, hoot*. "DAD! It is you!" I call out as we happily greet each other, both of us splashing around and hooting to each other. "Wait, Dad, I want you to meet my friend, Selina. We met on a lake we both visited during our migration here." "Good to meet you, Selina," my dad responds.

"Nice to meet you too, Dad?" Selina questions.

"My name is Oliver, but you can call me dad if you like," he says.

We all splash around and vocalize happily before making our way down into the cold ocean water to capture our morning meal. Together we feast on crayfish and other ocean creatures until our bellies are full.

Now it is preening time. I thought it was difficult on the lake but, goodness, the ocean water is so full of waves because it's very windy here. I really need to work at this. Selina and I do the best we can to preen ourselves gracefully. Dad, however, is a pro.

"Dad, I have some questions about the ocean environment. What are those loud sounding shapes that rumble in the water?" I begin to ask.

"They are different cargo ships carrying supplies through the area for people to use," Dad explains to me.

"And those tall fixtures with lights on them, what are they, Dad?" I continue asking.

"They are called lighthouses and are used as a guide for all the ships and boats out on the water. Lighthouses help the ships find land," Dad says sharing all that he has learned.

The day turns into night and as I begin to relax from all of the day's excitement, my mind starts to wander, "Dad, where is Momma? I miss her so much, and I really want Selina to meet her." Dad lowers his head and looks so unhappy. I have never seen him this way.

"Ray, I have not seen Momma since I have been here on the ocean and have been so saddened by the thought of you asking me about her. I fear her journey was not a successful one," he explains.

I look at my dad with sadness and anger. "NO! NO! NO! Dad please tell me we will find Momma!" Selina swims close to me to try to comfort me.

"I'm so sorry, Ray. I'm here for you. Please don't be so sad," Selina says as I nestle closer to her.

My dad swims to us, "Ray, it's going to be ok." I lower my bill into my feathers, close my eyes, and try to dream about the days I had with my momma.

The next morning I wake with a very sad heart knowing I will never be with Momma again. "Selina, Dad, I would like to spend some time on my own today if that is ok with you," I say.

"Go ahead, Ray," Dad approves, "Selina and I will be around. Call to us if you want our company or need anything." I watch as they swim away, and then I begin my search for Momma.

My belly rumbles so I know it's time to eat something first so I will have energy to find my momma. I dive down into the ocean, capture a crawfish, and gobble it down. I then dive down a second time and catch another. I feel satisfied for now.

I paddle and paddle and call out, " Momma, Momma," but there's no reply. I continue paddling and come close to an island with a lighthouse on it. I swim closer to shore and continue calling out for Momma, still with no reply. I'm heartbroken.

The sky begins to darken and big, black clouds move in. "Uh oh, I know what this means. A storm is about to hit just as it did on my home lake when I was younger," I say out loud. *Boom!* The sound of thunder is upon me. *Crash*! Flashes light up the darkened sky. The clouds open with a downpour of soaking, cold rain that quickly meets the tops of the waves.

I remember how Momma lowered her wing, eased me up onto her back, and brought me close to shore under the branches of an overhanging tree. There are no trees here, however, I find some rocks that I can huddle close to. I bunker down and briefly close my eyes. The wind howls fiercely, and the waves hit the rocks with great force. "Oh Momma, how I wish you were here with me. I'm so scared," I try to say but the wind mutes my voice.

CHAPTER 8

When I open my eyes, the storm begins to subside and the sun slowly begins to shine brighter and brighter. I hear a familiar voice. It sounds like Momma. My heart begins to fill with joy! " Momma, Momma is that you?" I exclaim.

"Yes, Ray, it is me," the voice says.

"But Momma, why can't I see you?"

"Ray, I'm not with you on earth any longer."

I feel a huge lump in my throat. "Momma, I love you, and I miss you. Please come back!"

"My time with you and Dad is over, and I am at rest now. Please go back to your dad and Selina."

"But Momma, how do you know about Selina?"

"From where I am Ray, high up in the sky at a place of rest, I can see you, your dad, Selina and so much more. Just know I will always be with you in your heart, and I will always be watching over you. Please paddle back to your Dad now."

"Okay, Momma, I will," I respond with a bit of hesitation.

I pause a moment to collect my thoughts. *OK, I can do this. I'm ready. It's time to head back.*

My mind is racing, trying to understand what has just happened. I paddle faster than I ever have retracing my original path. I remember that my dad said if I needed anything to call out. *Hoot, hoot, hoot. Hoot, hoot, hoot.* I call, but I don't hear a response.

As I continue to paddle, my tummy begins screaming at me for food. I turn my focus to satisfying my hunger. I peer down into the ocean and see nothing. It's just so cloudy . I continue peering down trying to refocus my eyes. Ah, there's one now! I dive as quickly as I can. Open wide! *Snap*! I grab it with my bill, surface, and swallow it down. That was so easy. Several more times I continue diving and feeding my belly until it is satisfied. Now I can continue on my journey.

I paddle on for a bit more and realize that the night sky is rolling in once again. When I ventured out on my search, it did not seem as if I had traveled this far. I try calling out again, *Hoot, hoot, hoot.* This time, I hear a faint *Hoot.* I continue paddling toward the response. *Hoot, hoot, hoot,* I reply again. A wail answers my call. It sounds like, "Where are you?"

I get so excited. It must be Dad and Selina. I let out a happy wail, "I am here!" I continue swimming toward their voices. Suddenly, before my eyes, I see two loons approaching, one is somewhat smaller than the other. I'm sure it is them. *Hoot, hoot, hoot,* I cry out excitedly.

Dad and Selina respond back as if they were singing a song of happiness in a syncopated rhythm with a series of hoots and wails. We are all happy to be back together.

CHAPTER 9

Winter was long and cold for Ray, Selina and Dad, however, they remained safe and happy on the ocean. During this time, they made many friends with other adult and juvenile loons. Salina spoke about her mother, Lyla, several times causing Dad to become interested in visiting Lake Massabesic to meet her.

On a spring morning in early April, the sun was shining with its bright warm yellow glow over the calm ocean waves. The smell of the clean salt water was in the air as it softly blew across the surface of its silent whitecaps. Selina and I were about to have our morning meal when Dad swam toward us calling *hoot, hoot, hoot.*

"Yes, Dad, what is it?"

"Well kids, it's time for me to leave you both and head back to Pawtuckaway Lake."

"Oh no, not this again! I'm going with you this time!"

"I'm sorry, Ray, but you, Selina, and all the other young loons ordinarily stay on the ocean until you are at least 2 years old. We adult loons return to our home lakes to breed and raise a new family. You and Selina are too young for that now, but your time will come."

"But Dad, how will you have a new family without Momma?"

"I will find a new mate to have a family with, but you will always be my son. That is just part of our life cycle."

I'm not at all liking what I am hearing, but I agree to Dad's wishes for now. We have our breakfast of crayfish together and when we are done, Dad chats with me briefly, "Ray, you have grown into a fine young loon, and I'm sure you will do well in life. Stay safe and take care of yourself and Selina until we meet again."

I watch as my dad makes his graceful take off up into the clear blue sky. He looks down at me and leaves with the sound of his tremolo echoing across the open ocean. I watch him as he becomes just a black speck in the sky, just as I had done that very last time I saw Momma. This time, however, I do not cry. I have other plans in mind.

CHAPTER 10

Selina and I go about our daily routine of eating, preening, and frolicking in the water. I'm trying to think of a clever way to slip away from Selina and start my journey back to Pawtuckaway Lake. I know what my dad told me, but I can't help how I feel. I'm not an ordinary young loon, so I will not stay on the ocean for two years.

The next morning while Selina and I are having breakfast, I ask, "Selina, how comfortable are you with the new friends we have made? I mean if something were to happen and I was not here with you, would you be ok with that?"

"I think I know you well enough to know that you are up to something, and whatever it is you are planning, I want in!" Selina replies.

"I don't want to put you in danger, so I feel it is best if you are not a part of my plan."

"Just tell me, and I will make my own decision, if you don't mind."

"OK! Fine! I'm going to head back to my birth lake to be with my dad."

"But your dad said we should stay on the ocean until we are older."

"I understand that, Selina, but in my heart, I feel it is the right thing to do."

"Well, if you go, I'm going too! Besides, I'm not as comfortable with our new friends as I am with you."
" You are making this difficult, Selina!"

"Ray, it wouldn't be difficult if you just agreed to let me come along with you. Remember how nice it was to have each other's company when we traveled here together? Wouldn't you like that better than traveling alone?"

"Now that you put it that way, Selina, it does give me something to think about."

"One last thing you may want to ask yourself is how your dad might feel knowing you left me here."

"I guess it's settled then. We head to Pawtuckaway Lake together!"

To be continued. Stay tuned for book 2.

ABOUT THE AUTHOR

Maria T. Moralez has always loved taking photographs and being outdoors. In 1982 she attended The New England School of Photography where she earned a Certificate in Photography. While raising her family Maria opened her own Licensed Family Child Care and helped other families with their childcare needs for nearly 20 years. During that time, she and her family spent numerous summer vacations at Pawtuckaway State Park in Nottingham, N.H. That is where her passion for loons truly began. Maria took many photographs of loons, nature, and wildlife at the park. She and her husband also volunteered for the Loon Preservation Committee observing, documenting and reported the information they gathered about the loons on the lake. In 2020 Maria began writing a children's book about loons. She knew she wanted to use all her own photographs to illustrate the book as well as include facts about loons to educate others. That is how Ray's Journey came to life.

I would like to thank my family and the Loon Preservation Committee (LPC) for their help and support through my writing journey.

Printed in the United States
by Baker & Taylor Publisher Services